The Life and Birdie Hayes

The Gift

Jeri Anne Agee

Illustrated by Bryan Langdo

Sky Pony Press
New York

Table of Contents

Chapter 1

SMALL TOWN, BIG NEWS

My name is Birdie Mae Hayes and I live in Rainbow, Alabama with my mama, daddy, and my little brother Bubba. I'm in third grade and my best friend, Sally Rose Hope, lives right down the street from me. I know, I know, it sounds like the perfect life, except that my little brother Bubba drives me crazy, and lately I can't stop feeling like something is about to happen. Or maybe like I'm waiting for something. I don't really know how to describe it. I asked Sally if she ever feels like she's waiting for something, and she said, "Waiting for what, like the bus or something?"

I haven't said anything to Mama about it because she would probably make me lie down or tell me it's a phase and I'll grow out of it. She's always saying Bubba will grow out of phases, like sucking his thumb or eating paper (well, he still eats paper sometimes but Mama says he will grow out of that eventually).

It's been six weeks since school started, and it's been pretty quiet around here. I mean, there have been a couple of little things, like when Bubba tried to clean off his feet in the toilet and got his foot stuck and the fire department had to come, or when Sally's cat pulled a chunk of her hair out. Sally got a real cute haircut to cover it up though and no one could tell anything had happened. Except for on the weekends when she just gets up and

comes over and her hair is still kind of sticking up and you can see a bald spot the size of a golf ball on the back of her head. Luckily, it's growing back pretty fast, I know because she asks me about fifty gazillion times a day if her bald spot is showing. I mean, I've heard Daddy ask Mama that before but not all day long, every single day.

I guess the biggest news to hit our town since the movie theater got a second screen is that someone is finally moving into old lady Miller's house. Old lady Miller lived in that house by herself for as long as I can remember. Well, by herself if you don't count about fifty cats. I'm just guessing it was about fifty because every time Sally and I would walk by her house we would try to count the ones we could see. We usually counted around twenty-five or so. We thought if we could see twenty-five cats there's got to be at least another twenty-five we can't see.

Anyway, Mama said that old lady Miller got too old to take care of herself and her cats so she moved in with her son and his family. I sure hope they like cats!

At church last Sunday all the talk was about the new family moving into old lady Miller's house. You would think it was the Queen of

England moving to Rainbow. Sally's mama and daddy told my mama and daddy their last name is Doolittle and they have a girl who's close to Bubba's age and a boy about our age. If that's true and he's in third grade he'll be in either Miss Flowers's class or Mrs. Crumbly's class.

Miss Flowers and Mrs. Crumbly are the only two third-grade teachers and they are about as opposite as you can get. Miss Flowers is young and really sweet and Mrs. Crumbly is old and kind of grumpy. Well, I don't really know if she's grumpy or not. She's never said anything to me but whenever I see her, she looks like a mad grandma. And I can hear her yelling at her class through the wall sometimes.

Sally was real happy when she found out we got Miss Flowers instead of Mrs. Crumbly. Sally's brother Darrel had Mrs. Crumbly two years ago and she didn't want to be the one to remind Mrs. Crumbly of when Darrel put a piece of gum on her chair! Yep, she sat in it. Then she threatened to give the entire class extra homework for two weeks if someone didn't come forward. Sally said Darrel admitted it right away because he would pick getting in trouble over extra homework any day.

But if there is a new boy coming to our school anytime soon, no one seems to know anything about it, and no one has moved into old lady Miller's house yet. I guess this feeling I'm having could be because of a new boy? But I sure hope it's a lot more exciting than that. Mama says that sometimes you need to listen to your gut, and right now my gut is telling me that things are about to get a lot more interesting in my life.

Chapter 2

LUNCHROOM DISASTER

A few days later, there was a big moving truck in front of old lady Miller's house. Sally and I tried to watch as much as we could without being too obvious. We must have ridden our bikes back and forth in front of their house for over an hour and we still didn't see anyone other than the movers. We never saw a mom or dad or any kids.

Even the next morning when we got on the bus and stopped near the Miller house, only the usual kids were waiting. There wasn't a new kid in the bunch.

Then finally during the morning announcements, the principal, Mr. Green, announced, "Today is a special day because we have a new student. His name is Peter Doolittle Jr. and he is in Mrs. Crumbly's third grade class. I want everyone to give him a warm Rainbow Elementary welcome!"

I'm sure Peter Doolittle Jr. was already nervous enough on his first day at a new school without having Mr. Green tell everybody his name and whose class he's in. I bet every kid in Mrs. Crumbly's class was staring a hole through him.

That day at lunch Sally and I were in the lunch line trying to decide between the Salisbury steak or the chicken nuggets when we saw a big crowd around one of the lunch tables. All I could see was Virginia Flanker in the middle of it all. It's not hard to see her because she's about six feet tall and her ponytail is up so high it makes her seem even

taller! She still wears a dress to school every day but at least she hasn't chased any of the boys around trying to kiss them this year . . . yet. She's best friends with Doyle Baker, who's in fourth grade. He is pretty much the school bully and is always trying to embarrass the younger kids. He and Virginia are friends because the Flankers and the Bakers have

lived next door to each other since they were
little. I don't know if Doyle's meanness rubbed
off on Virginia or if Virginia's meanness
rubbed off on Doyle. Last year at the school
carnival on the last day of school, Sally and
I waited in the snow cone line forever. As
soon as we got our snow cones Virginia came
running up behind us and "accidentally"

tripped and fell into us. We both dropped
our snow cones in the dirt, upside down,
of course. She said, "Oops, I didn't see you
there!" and ran away laughing.

I was still thinking about my grape and
cherry snow cone falling in the dirt when Sally
elbowed me in the side because Miss Percy, our
lunchroom lady, was asking me if I wanted the
Salisbury steak or the chicken nuggets. Sally
and I both decided on the Salisbury steak,
mashed potatoes with extra gravy, and two

rolls with extra gravy to dip them in. We both *really* like gravy.

As we were walking over to our table I finally saw what all the fuss was about. There was a crowd of kids around a boy I'd never seen before. I was trying to get a better look when he turned his head and looked right at me. I could feel my face getting red. I wasn't paying attention to where I was going and didn't notice that Sally had stopped walking. I walked right into the back of her and all I

can say is *huge gravy mess*! Not only did I hit
Sally in the back with my tray but my plate
slid off my tray and right onto my shirt. Well,
of course Sally let out a scream as soon as
I smacked her in the back with my tray and
everyone in the lunch room turned around
to see what happened. The only thing I

remember after that is the boy I'd never seen before handing me a big stack of napkins. He was tall with red hair and blue eyes, and that's when I realized it must be Peter Doolittle. After that it was just a blur of lunch ladies and mops and Miss Flowers helping me get cleaned up in the bathroom. She left for a minute and came back in with a T-shirt from the lost and found. She said it was the best she could find. It was lime green and said I BROUGHT THE AWESOME, WHAT DID YOU BRING?

Thank goodness it's Friday, I thought.

Chapter 3

THE NEW KID

Peter Doolittle still wasn't on the bus after school that day.

"Maybe he doesn't know all the kids ride the bus around here," I said to Sally. Sally wiped the sweat from her forehead and pulled out her paper fan and said, "Well, I don't know where he's going to sit if he does start riding the bus; we're already packed in here like sardines."

We went to my house so I could change out of the I BROUGHT THE AWESOME, WHAT DID YOU BRING? T-shirt. Then we grabbed a snack and decided to walk over to the park before dinner. We were sitting in our usual swings when Sally's brother Darrel, who's in fifth grade, rode his bike right between us and pushed us both so we were swinging sideways and crashed into each other.

Sally yelled, "Darrel, I'm telling Mama if you don't stop bothering us every time we're up here!"

He just ignored her and kept riding his bike straight into the woods until we couldn't see him anymore. There's a hiking trail in the woods with a tree house back there that kids play in sometimes.

We were just staring at where Darrel had ridden his bike into the woods and didn't hear anyone walk up.

"Hey!" we heard a voice say.

We both screamed.

Peter Doolittle Jr. said, "Sorry, I didn't mean to scare you."

Sally exclaimed, "You can't just sneak up on people like that. You almost gave us a heart attack!"

I realized who he was and said, "Hey, you must be the new kid. I'm Birdie Mae, and this is Sally."

He said, "I'm Peter. We just moved in down the street."

Sally said proudly, "Yeah, we know who you are—everybody knows. This is a pretty small town if you haven't noticed. We were

wondering why you didn't ride the bus today. And are there any cats living in your house? And is Mrs. Crumbly really a mean teacher? And—"

"Sally, stop asking him so many questions!" I said.

Peter laughed and said, "That's okay. I don't mind. I wasn't on the bus today because it was my first day and I had to go in early with my mom to fill out some papers and stuff, but I'll be riding the bus from now on. And I haven't seen any cats living in our house so far, and I haven't been in Mrs. Crumbly's class long enough to know if she's mean or not, but I'll let you know."

We talked for a little while longer until we heard some hoots and hollers and laughter coming from the woods where Darrel had ridden his bike.

Peter asked, "What's going on in there?"

"Darrel, Sally's brother, rode his bike in there and there's probably some kids playing around on the tree house back there," I said.

Peter exclaimed, "There's a tree house? Let's go see what's going on!"

Sally and I just looked at each other because neither of us had ever actually been to the tree house. We'd never even walked far enough back in the woods to get a glimpse of it. But we both shrugged our shoulders, and the three of us started walking that way.

Chapter 4

THE TREE HOUSE

It seemed like the longer we walked the bigger the trees got and the smaller the trail got. I was beginning to wonder if we took the wrong trail when we rounded a corner and walked into a clearing. Right there standing in the middle was the biggest tree I've ever seen. There were two bikes leaning against the bottom of the tree, and at the very top was a huge purple tree house with a bright green door. We looked up and there was Darrel with the school bully, Doyle Baker. Darrel was on the roof of the tree house leaning way out, trying to grab a rope that was tied to a tree branch. The tree house looked like it was about a hundred years old and might fall out of that tree any minute.

Doyle looked up at Darrel and yelled, "Hey, I said I was going first!" and grabbed Darrel's leg and almost made him fall.

Darrel yelled back, "Hold your horses, I want to make sure the rope is tied tight enough."

Peter looked at us and whispered, "I don't know what they're planning on doing, but I sure hope it doesn't have anything to do with swinging off the top of that tree house."

Just then I felt it—the feeling again, like butterflies in my stomach, but extra butterflies. Like something was about to happen . . . but it was different. It was stronger than usual, and it was starting to make me feel nervous.

Sally looked at me and asked, "Birdie Mae, what's wrong? You look like you're going to be sick or something!"

That's when it happened: I closed my eyes for a second, and I saw a vision of Doyle Baker falling out of the tree and landing on the ground. Before I knew what was happening or why, I yelled, "DON'T DO IT!" at the top of my lungs.

Sally and Peter both jumped when I yelled and then everything got quiet and everyone, including Darrel and Doyle, was staring at me.

"Whoa!" exclaimed Sally. "What's gotten into you?"

Before I could say anything, Darrel hopped down off the roof of the tree house and said, "The roof is pretty bad but the real problem is that branch. I don't think it's strong enough to hold anyone swinging on that rope."

Darrel may ride his bike like a crazy person and get in trouble at school, but he's not going to do something dumb like swing from a rope off the top of a tree house, I thought.

Just then, Doyle pushed Darrel aside and climbed up on top of the tree house anyway. He gave the rope a couple of tugs, chuckled, and said, "It feels fine to me. Maybe you're just a big chicken."

Darrel looked at Doyle for a long time and just shook his head and said, "Doyle, it's a bad idea, but I'm not your mama and I can't tell you what to do." And then he climbed down the ladder and walked over to where we were standing.

Doyle just laughed and yelled, "What are you, the tree house police or something?"

Before anyone could say another word, he grabbed the rope and swung way out from the roof of the tree house. We heard a loud crack, and then we saw Doyle Baker fall and hit the ground. It happened so fast we didn't know what to do. He sat up slowly, looked over at us, grabbed his ankle, and started crying like a baby. We ran over, and Darrel and Peter helped him up and dusted him off.

He tried to walk, and started crying even harder.

Darrel has a big box strapped to the front of his bike that he uses to carry around all sorts of things. Last summer he found five puppies by the river, so he loaded them up in his box and rode around town with them until he found each one of them a good home. I guess today he planned on using it to carry Doyle, because he and Peter lifted Doyle up and squeezed him down into the box. Once he was in there, his knees were touching his chin and all you could see was his head and the bottom of his legs sticking out. I was wondering if they would ever get him back out.

With Doyle crammed in the box, still crying like a baby, Darrel hopped on his bike and took off. He was pedaling so fast we had to run to try to keep up with him. Just as we

came out of the woods we caught a glimpse of them at the bottom of the hill heading toward Doyle's house.

Peter, Sally and I just stood there looking down the hill. Then Peter said, "Birdie Mae, why did you yell for Doyle not to jump?"

I guess Sally wanted to know the answer too because she turned around and looked at me and said, "Yeah, you're usually not such a worrywart, what was that all about?"

I said, "I don't know, it just didn't look safe and I thought somebody might get hurt." I didn't want to get into the whole thing in front of Peter.

Sally said, "Of course someone was going to get hurt. No one should be up on that old thing, much less trying to swing like a monkey from a tree. You and Darrel both told him not to do it and he still did. He's not the sharpest crayon in the box, if you know what I mean."

Then Peter said, "Well, I hope he's okay. I guess I better be getting home. I'll see you at school on Monday."

Once he was gone, I looked around to make sure Sally and I were alone and then I whispered, "Sally, something really strange just happened to me back there."

She said, "Yeah, I was there. You looked like you might throw up and then you yelled at the top of your lungs and then Doyle Baker fell from the sky and crashed to the ground."

I said, "But I think I knew it was about to happen. You know how I asked you if you ever have a feeling like you're waiting for something?"

She said, "Yeah, like when we wait for Christmas?"

I said, "Yes, but it feels more like waiting for something to happen. I just don't know what or when. But just now when we were in the woods I started feeling funny and I closed my eyes for just a second and I had a vision of Doyle Baker falling from that tree and hitting the ground. That's why I yelled like I did."

Sally just stared at me for a long time. Then she walked over to our swings and sat down and started swinging. I joined her.

We were swinging in silence for a minute when Sally said, "Well, I think we all knew something bad was going to happen when they tied that rope to the branch. Your feeling was probably what we were all feeling. It was dangerous and someone could get hurt and they did."

I was hoping Sally was right, but I knew there was more to it. I had a feeling that something was about to happen—and then I saw it happen before it did.

Sally was quiet for a few seconds and then said, "Or I guess there's always the chance you can see into the future."

I started laughing, nervously, because I was just thinking the same thing and I wasn't sure how I felt about it.

Sally said, "Why does all the cool stuff always happen to you?"

We both laughed and then we jumped off our swings and headed home for dinner.

When I was washing up for dinner, I couldn't stop thinking about what Sally had said in the park about me being able to see into the future. That seemed to be exactly what had happened, if you ask me. I had a vision of Doyle Baker falling out of that tree just seconds before it really happened.

Chapter 5

BOUNCY PONY RIDE

When I walked into the kitchen, dinner was already on the table and I heard Mama say, "I'm sure it's going to be fine, Jim, they seem real nice."

Daddy said, "Patsy, you think everybody is nice and maybe they are, but right this minute I don't like 'em!"

As I sat down at the table Mama said, "Okay, suit yourself, you big ole baby," and hit Daddy over the head with a dish rag. He didn't look up, but I could see he was trying not to smile.

Even so, I could tell Daddy was grumpy by the way he was acting. After we said the blessing, I asked Daddy how his day was.

He answered, "Well, Birdie Mae, let me tell you how my day was. It turns out our new neighbors down the street, the Doolittles, just bought the other grocery store in town. And this weekend, all weekend long, they're having a—a big—well, I guess a big grocery store party is what you'd call it!"

For as long as I can remember there's ever only been two grocery stores in town. One that's been closed for years and then the one that Daddy owns. So basically, Daddy's store was the only grocery store around until now.

"What's a grocery store party?" I asked.

He answered, "That's a good question, because grocery stores are for buying groceries, not for parties with face painting and bouncy houses and pony rides!"

I guess that got Bubba's attention. He was sitting in his booster seat pretending that his fish stick was a rocket blasting off when he heard Daddy say "bouncy houses and pony rides."

Bubba started chanting "I go bouncy pony ride, I go bouncy pony ride," over and over again as he was making a long piece of asparagus bounce around his plate.

I think we all looked over at him so quickly because we could actually understand what he was saying. Usually he has his pacifier in his mouth but it was lying beside his plate and he had a big smile on his face, still chanting "I go bouncy pony ride," and then he made his asparagus rear up like a horse and said "Neigh . . . neigh . . . whoa bouncy pony ride!"

Daddy stood up and said, "Well that's just great, now Bubba wants to go to the grocery store party. The next thing you know the whole town will be there going 'bouncy pony ride' and buying all of their groceries from there too!"

I didn't think now was the best time to tell Daddy I had met Peter Doolittle Jr. Daddy took his plate into the kitchen and mumbled something about working in the garage for a little while.

We heard the garage door open and close, and Mama said, "Birdie Mae, what you just witnessed is what it looks like for a thirty-eight-year-old man to have a temper tantrum like a baby."

Bubba then changed his chant from "I go bouncy pony ride" to "Daddy baby, Daddy baby!" Mama and I laughed, and then he grabbed three pieces of asparagus and stuffed them all in his mouth at once.

I told Mama, "I met Peter Doolittle Jr. today and he's really nice, and maybe Daddy will like Mr. Doolittle, once he gets to know him. Maybe they'll be friends and they can do fun grocery store stuff together!"

Mama smiled and said, "Well, I took some cookies over to the Doolittle's today and met Mrs. Doolittle, and we got along just fine, too. We were a little nervous about meeting each other with the whole grocery store situation. I told her that your daddy is stubborn as a mule and as competitive as they come. Unfortunately, she said Mr. Doolittle is exactly the same way."

Mama told me how nice Mrs. Doolittle is and that they have a little girl the same age as Bubba named Isabella, they call her Izzy. She said Bubba and Izzy really hit it off.

Mama said, just loud enough to get Bubba's attention, "Izzy doesn't take a pacifier, she never did, and she stopped taking a baby bottle about a year ago. I'm hoping Bubba will decide he doesn't need a pacey or a bottle since Izzy doesn't need one."

Bubba stared at her for a few seconds and slowly reached over and grabbed his pacifier and put it in his lap and then went back to shoving more food in his mouth.

Then she told me about how Izzy drinks out of a sippy cup and how Bubba tried to do the same thing today, only it wasn't a sippy cup, it was Mama's cup of iced tea, and he poured it all down the front of his shirt. Izzy thought it was hilarious and we know how Bubba likes to make people laugh so Mama and Mrs. Doolittle had to go around and make sure there weren't any other cups sitting around that he could pour all over himself.

Mama also said that the Doolittles were having a Halloween party at their house next Friday so they could get to know some of their new neighbors.

Then Mama looked at me for a few seconds and reached over and put the back of her hand to my forehead.

She asked, "Are you feeling all right? You look a little tired."

I was just about to tell her everything that had happened that day when the phone rang and she got up to answer it.

Chapter 6

CALL FROM MRS. BAKER

When Mama answered the phone I could hear bits and pieces of her conversation.

I heard her say, "Oh my, is he all right?"

I quietly inched my way closer to the hall, so I could hear a little better.

There was a long pause and then Mama said, "Yes, Mrs. Baker, I completely understand. Now let me see if I've got this straight. Your son, Doyle, was about to swing like Tarzan from a rope that was tied to a branch at the top of that old rickety tree house, when Birdie Mae saw him and tried to stop him? But then

Doyle decided to do it anyway, and that's when he fell and broke his foot?"

I covered my mouth with my hand so I wouldn't laugh out loud. Then I heard Mama say, "No, not at all, thank *you*, Mrs. Baker, and I do hope Doyle gets his cast off real soon, bless his heart." And then she hung up the phone.

I tiptoed back over to the sink with a smile on my face, wondering if Mrs. Baker was still standing there in shock with the phone in her hand. When Mama came back into the kitchen I couldn't help but look at her with wide eyes. She walked over and took the plate I was holding out of my hand and started drying it.

She said, "If we hurry up with the dishes I think we can catch the end of *Wheel of Fortune*."

I stood there for a minute, waiting for Mama to ask me about Doyle Baker, but she never did.

Finally, I said, "Mama, do you ever get a feeling like something is about to happen before it happens?"

Mama looked over at me with a curious expression and was about to say something when Bubba ran into the kitchen, naked as a jaybird, with a pacey in his mouth and two in each hand. I scooped him up and he started giggling and squirming.

I walked into the living room and put him down. He looked at me with a sneaky little grin and slowly turned his back to me. Then he stuck his bottom out toward me and let out a long toot and ran down the hall toward his room giggling his little head off.

"*Mama*, Bubba tooted at me again!" I cried.

"Well, Birdie Mae, he is a boy, and he's only two years old. It's probably just a phase, and he'll grow out of it. Why don't you go ahead and turn on the *Wheel*?"

Chapter 7

FLYING TATER TOTS

On Monday morning when Daddy was leaving for work, Mama said, "Oh, Friday night the Doolittles are having a Halloween party and I said we'd go—it starts at seven o'clock, right after trick or treating."

Daddy stopped walking and just stood there facing the door with his back to us. He didn't turn around; he just stood there staring at the door. I guess Mama and I had both been holding our breath because when Daddy opened the door and said, "Okey dokey, I'll see everyone this afternoon," and closed it, Mama and I both let out a breath. She said, "Well, that went better than I expected!"

At school, everyone was talking about the Doolittles' party on Friday night, even Virginia Flanker and Doyle Baker. I wasn't thrilled that they would be there, but at least we'd all be dressed up in costumes, so maybe I wouldn't recognize them.

During lunch, Peter, Sally, and I were sitting at a table talking about the party when a tater tot came out of nowhere and landed right on top of my pudding.

We all turned around and there was Doyle Baker sitting next to Billy Simmons, stacking tater tots

on top of Billy's book and wearing Billy's glasses. Billy Simmons is quiet and sweet and would never hurt a fly. We've been in the same class since kindergarten and he's shy at first, but when you get to know him he's really funny and definitely the smartest kid in school. There he was just sitting there, not doing or saying anything, just minding his own business.

Doyle picked up another tater tot and threw it across the room at another table. Doyle just laughed and said "Two points" when the tater tot bounced off a first grader's head and into his lunch box.

Everyone just stared at him.

Before I knew what was happening, Peter was out of his seat and standing over Doyle like a red-headed giant.

Doyle had a cast on his foot but he stood up and took two wobbly steps toward Peter until he was just a few inches from his face.

The next thing you know, about a dozen
kids are standing around us.

Peter said, "Doyle, I've only been here for a
week, and all I've seen you do is bully people.
Give Billy his glasses back."

Doyle said those two words; those dreaded two words that I think we all knew he'd say.

"MAKE ME!"

It's too bad I couldn't make myself have another vision about Doyle Baker because I really wanted to know if we should get out of the way or not.

Peter was quiet for a second. I could tell he was trying to figure out what to do next.

I felt bad for Peter so I stood up and said, "Doyle, you better listen to him because Sally's mama told my mama that Peter got kicked out of his last school for beating up a kid who was bullying another kid. Yep, and she hopes it doesn't happen again but she's afraid it might, because Peter has such a bad temper."

Peter and Doyle were both looking at me and Peter opened his mouth like he was going to say something but then he closed it and looked down at Doyle and said, "And after you give Billy his glasses back you can start cleaning up those tater tots too!"

They stood there staring at each other for a few seconds. Peter seemed to get even taller and Doyle seemed to get smaller. Then, of all things, Billy Simmons stood up on his chair and reached over and took his glasses off of Doyle's face and then sat back down. Doyle looked around, and then he turned to walk out, but before he did he swiped the tater tots off of Billy's book right onto the cafeteria floor.

This was not Doyle's lucky day, because just as the last tater tot hit the floor, Mrs. Crumbly was standing right next to him.

She barked, "What in the world is going on here? Have you all lost your minds? You are acting like a bunch of circus clowns. And Doyle Baker, I'll let you pick the tater tots up before you go visit the principal's office. And while you're having a nice long visit with Mr. Green, I'll find out just how much help these nice people who work in the cafeteria could use. I'll make sure to have a long list of things for you to do every day after school for the next two weeks. And I believe I heard Miss Percy mention a lost retainer, so grab some gloves on your way back from Mr. Green's office. Now everyone get back in your seats and finish your lunch. You've got five minutes until the bell!"

Everyone scattered, and Doyle just stood there. For a second it looked like he and Mrs. Crumbly were having a staring contest. If they were, then Mrs. Crumbly won because Doyle

started hopping around like a one-legged bunny picking up tater tots.

Sally, Peter, and I sat back down at our table and Billy picked up his tray and his book and came over and sat down with us.

Billy said, "Thanks, no one's ever stood up for me like that before."

"It's no big deal. Somebody should have stood up to him a long time ago," Peter said.

Then Sally blurted out, "Is that really why you moved here? Because you beat up a kid and they kicked you out of school?"

Peter and I started laughing and Billy and Sally just looked at us.

Peter said, "No, but it sounded pretty good, didn't it? I'm glad Birdie Mae could think of something to say because I sure couldn't. I've never been in a fight and I don't plan on being in one, but Doyle Baker doesn't have to know that."

We all laughed, and I knew from that moment on, the four of us were going to be thick as thieves, whatever that means. I heard Mama say it once about her and her friends from high school, so I guess it means best friends or something like that? Hopefully that's what it means and it doesn't mean we're going to go around stealing stuff.

Later that night, Daddy built a bonfire in our fire pit behind the house and we had a marshmallow roast and made s'mores with the neighbors. Everybody gets into the spirit of things around Halloween.

After we were stuffed with roasted marshmallows and tucked into bed, I still couldn't stop thinking about seeing Doyle Baker fall out of that tree. It had to just be a coincidence. It was silly to think it was anything different.

Chapter 8

THE FIRE

That night, I tossed and turned and dreamed about a fire in my backyard. In the dream, there was so much smoke, and I could just see the flicker of flames inching closer to the back of the house.

Suddenly, I was wide awake, and I had a strong feeling that something was about to happen—but this time, I was also afraid. And my feeling was worse than before—more urgent—and I honestly felt like I could throw up at any moment. Then, in my mind, I saw another vision: I saw my backyard on fire, just like in my dream. I jumped out of bed and ran to my parents' room.

"Daddy, Daddy!" I said, shaking his shoulder and trying to wake him. "DADDY!" I yelled. He sat up with a jolt and so did Mama.

"What is it? What's the matter?" he asked.

"I think the backyard is on fire! I have a bad feeling that the backyard is on fire, and I had a dream that the backyard is on fire so I think you should check on it now!" I cried.

Daddy sighed. "Birdie, it was just a bad dream, now go on back to bed."

Mama looked at me with a strange expression and then back at Daddy and said, "Jim, go check the backyard."

"But Patsy . . ." he grumbled.

Mama raised her voice just a little and said, "Jim, please go check the backyard now!"

Just then, we heard the wind whirling outside like a storm was coming, and Daddy got out of bed and walked to the back window. He looked out into the backyard and started mumbling something about marshmallows while he ran over to the side of the bed to put his slippers on.

I thought, why in the world is Daddy thinking about marshmallows at a time like this? Then it hit me—we roasted marshmallows earlier in the *fire pit* in the backyard!

I ran over to the window just in time to see a small fire flaring up in the grass next to the turned-over fire pit.

Daddy said, "Patsy, there's a fire in the backyard near the house! Get Bubba, and you three go out the front door until I tell you it's safe to come back inside."

I said, "Daddy, be careful and if things get out of control don't forget to stop, drop, and roll!" Even though I was scared, I was still pretty proud of myself for remembering what they taught us in school about what to do in a fire.

We did as Daddy said. Mama grabbed Bubba up out of his bed, and he just kept on sleeping on her shoulder. When we'd been outside for only about two minutes, Daddy came around to the front of the house and said, "Everything's fine now. It looks like I didn't put out all of the embers in the fire pit after we roasted marshmallows earlier, and the wind turned it over. It's been just dry enough around here to catch the grass on fire."

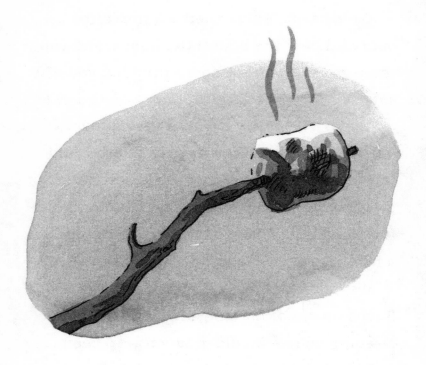

Daddy looked at me and asked, "Birdie Mae, how did you know about the fire? Did you smell smoke? Did you look out the window?"

I wasn't exactly sure how to answer this, because I didn't want Mama and Daddy to think I was crazy. So I looked down at my feet so I wouldn't have to see their expressions and said, "I had a dream about it, and when I woke up I had a bad feeling that something was going to happen, and then I saw a vision of the fire in the backyard."

I looked up to see Mama and Daddy looking at each other, not at me. Then Mama said, "It's time, Jim . . . It's time for Birdie Mae to visit with Grandma Mae for a couple of days, starting tomorrow." Grandma Mae is my daddy's mama, and I'm named after her.

Daddy looked at Mama for a long time, and they seemed to have a conversation without using any words. He nodded his head in agreement, and the next thing I knew it was planned that I was going to Grandma Mae's house in the morning! I love going to my Grandma Mae's house, and I would normally be really excited to see her, but I had no idea why I needed to visit so soon. I was even missing school for it. I was a little worried, because I had a feeling my visit had something to do with my visions. But how in the world could any of that be connected to my Grandma Mae?

Chapter 9

THE GIFT

The next morning it was decided that Mama would drive me to Grandma Mae's house because Daddy had to work. We left early in the morning—in fact, we got there so early that the second I stepped into the house, I could smell breakfast in the air. Grandma Mae said, "Birdie Mae, I cooked eggs, bacon, grits, and biscuits because I know that's your favorite."

Mama and I sat at the table and we all had breakfast while we talked for a while. After about an hour Mama said she had to go and that she would pick me up tomorrow. Grandpa said he needed to run some errands in town, and he walked Mama out.

So there I was, sitting at the table while Grandma Mae cleaned up the kitchen. I didn't really know why I was there. I mean, I always like to visit my grandparents, but this was the first time it was just me and Grandma Mae and definitely the first time I've missed school for a visit.

Then she sat down next to me and said, "Your mama told me you asked her if she ever gets a feeling like something is about to happen."

I said, "Yes, ma'am. Why, does it mean something bad and Mama and Daddy were too afraid to tell me so they brought me over here so you could tell me?"

Grandma Mae chuckled and replied, "No, sweetheart, it doesn't mean anything bad, and the reason you're here is because I also

occasionally get a feeling when something is about to happen, and so did your Great-great-grandmother Edith and your Great-great-great-great-grandmother Ida."

Then she looked at me and smiled and said, "You see, Birdie Mae, you were born with a gift."

I just looked at her for a few seconds and said, "Well, where is it? I'm almost nine years old, and nobody's given it to me yet!"

She laughed and said, "No, Birdie Mae, it's a gift inside of you. It's called clairvoyance, or some say it's like having a sixth sense. It means that sometimes, you may be able to see into the future. It can take time before you begin to recognize the feelings, and it can be confusing and a little scary. It may be that you suddenly feel anxious or excited or even have a feeling of waiting for something to happen. Sometimes, it may come to you in a dream."

I immediately thought about Doyle Baker and the fire in the backyard.

"Grandma, are you telling me the feeling I get like something is about to happen and the visions I see in my head are a gift? Can I give it back?" I asked.

She laughed again and said, "No, sweetie pie, it's not a gift you can give back, but I can promise you it isn't a bad thing. Over time it will get easier, and you will do good things with it."

The rest of the afternoon and that night Grandma Mae told me all about when she was close to my age and found out she had the gift and how she has had to learn to let things come to her and not always be waiting to feel something or see something. She also said each person who has the gift is different and special in their own way, and that my strange feelings were the gift telling me to pay attention because something was about to happen.

I asked her if Daddy knew about it, and why didn't he have it? She said, "Yes, your daddy knows about it. But so far it's only been women in our family who have it, and it also seems to skip a generation. When I was just a little younger than you are now, my mama took me over to visit my Grandma Edith and she and I had a talk just like this."

"So, is it sort of like a secret club that only me and a bunch of grandmas are in?" I asked.

She smiled. "Well, I guess that's one way of looking at it."

Grandma and I sat there for hours talking and telling stories. She ordered pizza and we ate it sitting right on the living room floor. I told her all about the fire last night and about the day Doyle Baker broke his foot. She said that if Doyle Baker wasn't so hardheaded he probably wouldn't be sitting at home right now with a broken foot.

I couldn't really argue with that.

That night my mind was still racing with more questions, and I had a hard time falling asleep. Being able to see things before they happen is kind of a big deal, I thought. Grandma Mae seems so calm about it. Maybe I'll find out more tomorrow—she said she has a big day planned for us.

Chapter 10

RAINBOW PARK

The next morning, I woke up to the smell of bacon and to what sounded like an injured animal. I lay there for a minute until my stomach started growling and I realized the injured animal sound was just Grandpa blowing his nose. I hopped out of bed and headed for the kitchen.

Grandma Mae said, "Oh good, you're up! We've got some things to do in town today."

I'm pretty sure Grandma Mae's town only has a post office, a restaurant, and a sheriff's station, so when she said we had some things to do I just assumed we were going to the post office and to the Fried Green Tomato for lunch. But when we got in the car I noticed Grandma Mae was heading in the opposite direction.

"Are you taking me home, Grandma?" I asked.

"Oh no, dear, I thought we'd do a little shopping in Rainbow, maybe stop for ice cream, and take a stroll around Rainbow Park," she said.

After we went into just about every store on Main Street, and Grandma Mae talked to just about every person we saw, we finally made our way over to the Dairy Dip for a double scoop of mint chocolate chip ice cream. From there, we walked over to the park, carefully balancing our giant ice cream cones.

Rainbow Park is right in the middle of downtown Rainbow, Alabama. It's lined so thick with magnolia and dogwood trees that it almost looks like a small forest growing right

in the middle of town. In the spring when
the dogwoods are in full bloom and the wind
blows, it looks like it's snowing. All four sides
of the park have tall arched entryways with
jasmine vines and white lights intertwined
through the arches. There are benches lining
the sidewalks all through the park. There's a

playground on one side of the park and a big fountain in the center.

As we walked, Grandma Mae took my hand and held it in hers.

We were walking and talking and eating our ice cream when out of nowhere I had one of my feelings. I told her I felt like something

was going to
happen. She
looked a little
surprised at
first but then
she smiled
and whispered,
"Close your eyes,
Birdie Mae, and try to
clear your mind."

I wasn't sure how I was going to clear my
mind with all those cicadas making so much
noise and my mint chocolate chip ice cream
dripping down my arm. But I closed my eyes
and felt the warmth of Grandma Mae's hand,
and suddenly things seemed to go quiet.

"Do you hear or see anything?" she asked.

The butterflies in my stomach started
going crazy. Then I had a vision of a little girl
riding her tricycle into the grass and right

into a tree stump—causing her to fall off her tricycle, start wailing, and lose her pink teddy bear behind a bush.

I opened my eyes and just then a little girl on a tricycle rounded the corner. She had a pink teddy bear sitting in the basket on the front of her bike. She was giggling and looking back at her parents, and just as she passed us she smiled and waved and rang the little bell on her bike handlebars.

I knew I had to do something! I asked Grandma Mae to hold my ice cream and I quickly started walking toward the little girl and her parents. As I caught up, the little girl rode off the sidewalk onto the grass and was heading toward the tree stump. I started running to get in front of her. Just as she got close to the stump, I jumped on it and stopped her tricycle before she ran smack dab into it—which meant before she could fall and before her teddy bear could go flying in the air and land behind that big bush. I had prevented her accident!

Her mama and daddy came running up and thanked me over and over for stopping their little girl from crashing into that tree stump. The little girl was now busy playing with her teddy bear. I looked at Grandma Mae and smiled. After the little girl and her parents thanked me again, they left. Grandma Mae hugged me and said, "You did so good, I'm so proud of you!"

I said, "Grandma, that was kind of cool, if you know what I mean!"

Grandma Mae laughed and said, "I know exactly what you mean! Now we better get back home or your mama is going to send out a search party for us."

That night I slept like a rock and woke up feeling pretty darn good about things.

Chapter 11

HALLOWEEN

The rest of the week was quiet and I didn't get any strange feelings or visions—just feelings of excitement about Halloween coming up.

Finally it was Friday! Sally was leaning out the window of my bedroom hollering, "Birdie Mae, we need more trash!"

I said, "Hold on! I'm trying to find some mud and all I can find is dirt. Go look in Bubba's closet. He's probably got all kinds of stuff in there we can use for trash."

It was starting to get dark, and we had to hurry with our costumes so we could trick-or-treat before the party.

Bubba was already running around the house in his costume. He was dressed as a ghost with a bowtie and a mustache. Mama got one of those fake mustaches and glued it to the top part of Bubba's pacifier so when he had it in his mouth it looked just like he had a mustache. I wasn't sure why Mama put the bowtie and the mustache on his ghost costume until Mrs. Doolittle and Izzy showed up at the door. Izzy was also dressed up as a ghost but she had a pink bow on the top of her head and some big pink wax candy lips.

Mrs. Doolittle said, "I hope you all are ready to go trick-or-treating. Izzy is already on her second pair of lips. She decided to bite the entire bottom lip off the first pair and I've only got one more left."

Mama introduced Daddy to Mrs. Doolittle
and Izzy. I think Mrs. Doolittle was trying
extra hard to get Daddy to like her. Of course,
it didn't really help things when Izzy looked
at Daddy and said, "I smell corn dogs!" Then
she turned around and headed for the door.

Sally and I ran back into my room and put
our faces down in my pillow so no one could
hear us laughing. We were laughing because
it was true—about half the time Daddy comes
home from work, he smells just like corn

dogs! His office at the grocery store is right behind the deli and about three times a week they cook up those little bite-size corn dogs and give them out to customers. It makes his office and everything in it smells like corn dogs.

We heard Mama and Mrs. Doolittle leave with Bubba and Izzy.

When Sally and I were ready I yelled down the hall, "Daddy, close your eyes and don't open them until we tell you!"

We walked into the kitchen and stood in front of Daddy and I said, "Okay, you can open them now!"

He opened his eyes and he looked at us for a second and said, "Dagnabbit, I could have sworn I took all the trash out this morning!"

We all three started laughing. Daddy said, "I don't know how you two came up with this but I bet you won't be seeing anyone else wearing the same costumes."

Sally and I were pretty proud of ourselves. We were dressed up as bags of garbage. We took two big trash bags and cut out arm holes and leg holes, then stepped into them while wearing tights and long-sleeved shirts. We stuffed the bags full of wadded up paper after they were on, then tied some string around the top so it looked like the bag was tied up and ready to go into the garbage can. We rubbed mud and some of Mama's eye liner all over our faces like dirt, and then Sally got one of those little snack bags of potato chips and ate the chips and stuck the bag on her head. I decided to go with an empty toilet paper roll on my head.

We grabbed our pillowcases, the same ones we've been using on Halloween to put our candy in since we were little, and headed out the door. We stopped by Sally's house so her mama and daddy could take some pictures and then we caught up to Mama, Bubba, Mrs.

Doolittle, and Izzy so we could trick-or-treat with them. Mrs. Doolittle said Peter, Billy, and Darrel left her house about an hour ago to trick-or-treat. Sally and I looked at each other and we picked up the pace because we both knew that if Darrel had been out there for an hour, there was a good chance some houses were already out of candy!

Chapter 12

PETER, PETER THE PUMPKIN EATER

After about an hour, Mama was carrying Bubba and Mrs. Doolittle was carrying Izzy. Sally and I were tired of lugging around our giant pillow cases full of candy, so we all headed over to the Doolittles' for the party.

We stopped by our house to make sure Daddy was coming and found him sitting on the front porch eating a Snickers bar. At least he was smiling, so maybe he wasn't dreading going over there so much after all. Or it could be all the candy bars he just ate, because when he stood up there were about a dozen of those little wrappers flattened out on the chair. He grabbed them and stuffed them in his pocket real quick and looked over at us. Mama was talking to Mrs. Doolittle but Bubba pointed at Daddy and said, "Me some candy too!"

Mama said, "I know you want some candy, you can pick out something from your candy bag when we get to the party."

Daddy looked over at me and winked. I thought about all of the empty candy wrappers in my bag and felt a little guilty about eating so much of it.

When we got to the party, Mr. Doolittle met us at the door and took Izzy from Mrs. Doolittle and introduced himself to Mama and Daddy. Peter came in and told us that all of the kids were in the basement. As Sally and I were heading toward the basement door, I looked back and saw Mr. Doolittle shake Daddy's hand and give him a smack on the back and say, "I'm Peter Doolittle Sr. It's nice to meet you. I hear that you and I have something in common!"

I couldn't hear Daddy's response but I had a funny feeling come over me and my stomach started to hurt. I thought, oh no, not now . . . please don't let anything bad happen between Daddy and Mr. Doolittle! I closed my eyes really tight and waited for a few seconds but nothing happened. I thought about Grandma Mae and what all she told me about relaxing and clearing my mind to allow the visions to just come to me. I gave it one more chance and closed my eyes one more time, but saw nothing. Zilch. I took a deep breath and let it out slowly, then walked down the basement stairs to join the others.

Peter and Billy were playing ping-pong. Peter was dressed as a doctor and Billy was dressed as a businessman, complete with a suit, tie, mustache, and his own glasses. Sally said, "What's up, Dr. Doolittle? How's it going, Mr. Simmons?" and I laughed louder than I meant to. I guess it was because I was nervous. I didn't know what was going on upstairs with Daddy and Mr. Doolittle and my stomach was really starting to feel funny.

I looked around the room and the rest of the kids were either sitting around sorting their candy or playing video games. Darrel was playing a video game with two fifth grade girls, and they giggled every time he said or did anything. I guessed he hadn't shown them yet how he could burp the ABCs.

Then Virginia Flanker walked in dressed in a nurse's costume. For a second I thought I might throw up. I didn't know if it was because of my stomachache or because of her. She headed straight for Peter and said, "Oh my goodness, Peter, it's like we planned our costumes together! We have to get Mother to take a picture of us!"

Peter turned about as red as his hair and said, "Okay, maybe later . . . Billy and I are going to finish this game first." Then he turned back, and I saw him roll his eyes at Billy.

Just then Mrs. Doolittle called down and said, "Who's ready to bob for apples? And I hope you kids haven't eaten too much candy because I've made my special pumpkin cake!"

That got everyone's attention, and we all headed upstairs.

When we got up there the first thing I saw was Mr. Doolittle and Daddy over in the corner talking. Then I saw Bubba, who of course had stripped off his costume and was running around in his Spiderman underwear with his mustache pacifier in his mouth.

There was a table full of fruit and vegetables and cheese and crackers and all of the healthy stuff. There was another table over by Daddy and Mr. Doolittle that had the biggest pumpkin I'd ever seen on it. I looked closer and realized it was a cake! A giant cake that looked just like a giant pumpkin! Just then, Bubba ran by and I could see a cheese cube sticking out of his ear. I grabbed his hand and walked him over to Mama. I said, "Mama, Bubba's got a piece of cheese stuck in his ear."

She picked up Bubba and was trying to get the piece of cheese out of his ear but he kept wriggling and laughing. The harder she tried the harder he laughed and said, "Mama tickle me!"

Then I leaned in and whispered, "How are things going with Daddy and Mr. Doolittle?"

Before she could answer we heard a lot of commotion and people were crowding around the table with the giant pumpkin cake. We made our way over there and I couldn't believe what I saw. Why hadn't I had a vision about this? There was Mr. Doolittle, face down in the giant pumpkin cake—and there was Daddy, standing behind him with a shocked look on his face!

Chapter 13

NEW FRIENDS AND NEW BEGINNINGS

Mama said, "Oh no, please tell me your daddy didn't do that."

Mr. Doolittle stood up, and he had so much orange frosting on his face I wasn't sure he could breathe, much less see. Then he stretched his arms straight out like Frankenstein and said in a really scary voice, "Watch out! Here comes Peter, Peter the Pumpkin Eater!"

The little kids started screaming and
laughing and running around, and the adults
were laughing and trying to get out of the way.

Daddy was laughing too and came over
to me and Mama and said, "Well, that was
the craziest thing I've ever seen. We were

just standing there talking about doing a grocery store charity event together and he was asking me where I play golf, and the next thing I know, he turned around and smashed his face right into the giant pumpkin cake!"

Mrs. Doolittle came over with a big smile. She said, "In case you're wondering what's going on, he's done this for years. When he was a kid he really did fall into a big orange pumpkin cake and all the kids called him Peter, Peter the Pumpkin Eater for the rest of the year. When Peter Jr. was big enough to dress up for Halloween and trick or treat, we started hosting an annual neighborhood Halloween party. The first time my husband asked me to make a giant pumpkin cake with lots of orange icing I thought it was a cute idea. Then the first time he smashed his face into the giant pumpkin cake and stood up and yelled, 'Watch out! Here comes Peter, Peter the Pumpkin Eater,' I thought, well . . . he's lost his mind. When I saw how much fun he and the kids were having, it just kind of became a tradition."

They all laughed and then my parents followed Mrs. Doolittle and the other grown-ups into the living room so they could avoid the pumpkin cake massacre.

When I walked over to where Sally, Peter, and Billy were standing, Peter said, "You should be safe from flying cake and frosting over here."

Just then a big glob of orange frosting smacked him right in the face. We looked over and there was Mr. Doolittle, standing in the kitchen pointing at Peter and laughing. The next thing you know, everyone was throwing cake and orange frosting and the kitchen looked like a giant pumpkin bomb had gone off. I saw Virginia Flanker run by, her blond ponytail now bright orange. She didn't look very happy.

I looked over at Sally and I opened my mouth to say something but when I did all that came out was, "BURRRRRRRRRRP!"

It was maybe the loudest burp I've ever heard in my life! I looked around to see if anyone had noticed. Sally, Peter, and Billy

were all looking at me with their eyes wide and their mouths hanging open.

I laughed nervously. "EXCUSE ME! Wow, my stomach feels a lot better now!"

At that moment, I realized that the funny feeling I'd been having—which I'd thought was going to lead to a vision—was just that I needed to burp. Oops!

We all laughed and for the next few minutes, until the cake throwing was over, we sat there talking and laughing and eating frosting right off the kitchen counters, and the cabinets, and the refrigerator, and anywhere else we saw frosting land.

It was late when we left the Doolittles'. We walked home with Sally's family, and Darrel had Bubba on his shoulders. Bubba thinks that Darrel is the greatest thing since sliced bread and Darrel is always nice about it and plays with him. Bubba was still just wearing his Spiderman underwear, but now he also had orange spiky hair.

Sally and I lagged behind everyone else because we were still talking about the party.

She whispered, "So did you have any of your feelings tonight?"

"No, but I thought I was having one earlier," I said. "I was so worried about how Daddy and Mr. Doolittle would get along because of the whole grocery store thing. Luckily, I just needed to let out that giant burp! Did you hear that thing?"

Sally said, "Did I hear it? That was the loudest burp I've ever heard in my life! Too bad you didn't get a feeling that it was coming, or you could have made an announcement so *everyone* could have heard it!"

We were both still laughing about it when we got to Sally's driveway. We said goodnight

and then she stood there watching me walk
the rest of the way to my house.

When I got to my driveway, I turned around and yelled the same thing I do every day: "See you tomorrow, Sally Rose Hope!"

Sally yelled back, "See you tomorrow, Birdie Mae Hayes!"

And then we both went inside.

Later, after Mama had tucked me in, I was lying there thinking about my family and my friends and thinking about my new gift. I wasn't sure how often my gift would show itself, but I was positive that things were going to be real interesting from now on.

READ ON FOR A SNEAK PEEK AT THE NEXT ADVENTURE IN THE LIFE AND TIMES OF BIRDIE MAE HAYES!

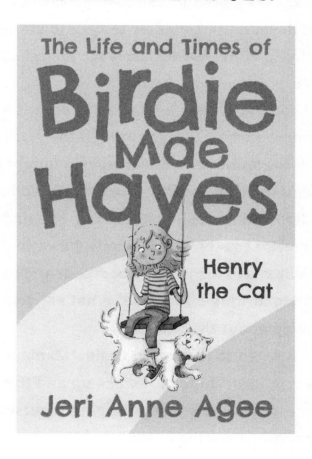

HENRY THE CAT

When I woke up on Saturday morning I wasn't expecting to find a big white fluffy cat sitting outside my bedroom window. But there he was. He stared at me, then he yawned, laid down on the window ledge and started cleaning himself. *Well just make yourself at home, why don't you*, I thought.

I got out of bed and walked over to the window. I watched him through the glass for a few minutes, wondering if he might be one of the cats left over from when Old Lady Miller lived in the neighborhood. She had at least fifty cats before she moved away.

Mama walked into my bedroom and said, "Good morning Birdie Mae! What are you looking at out the window?"

I pointed to the cat and said, "Mama, it's the strangest thing . . . I woke up and this big, white, fluffy cat is just sitting right outside my window staring at me."

Mama looked toward the window and then walked over to get a better look. I noticed her back stiffen a little and when she turned around she had a funny look on her face. She walked back across the room and sat on my bed.

She looked right at me and said, "Birdie Mae, are you telling me there is a big, white, fluffy cat sitting outside your window right now?

"Yes ma'am! Isn't he the cutest thing?" I asked.

Mama still had that same funny look on her face. She said, "Now, I don't want to upset you, but Birdie Mae, I don't see a big, white, fluffy cat outside your window. Or *any* cat outside your window. But I do believe *you* see a big white fluffy cat outside your window. I just think you may be the only one who can see it." She paused. My mouth had dropped open. "It sounds like I need to call Grandma Mae right away. I'll be right back."

And just like that, Mama got up, turned around, and left my bedroom in a hurry. I just stared at the bedroom door and then back at the cat over and over again. I started getting a nervous feeling, and I knew this all had something to do with my gift—or what mama now calls my "special abilities." That had to be the only reason Mama was calling Grandma Mae.

I could hear Mama talking on the phone but I couldn't hear what she was saying. Then, before I knew it, she was coming back down the hall. She rounded the corner to my room and said in a cheerful voice, "How about we take a ride out to Grandma Mae's house today?"

I immediately thought to myself, *Oh great . . . here we go again.*

ABOUT THE AUTHOR

Jeri Anne Agee grew up in Huntsville, Alabama, and graduated from the University of Alabama with a bachelor's degree in communications. An avid reader and a mother of three, Jeri Anne retired early from the financial industry, and at the age of forty-four, began writing her first children's book. Her quest to combine her own stories of growing up in the South with a character who is strong, lovable, loyal, and funny resulted in Birdie Mae Hayes. Jeri Anne currently resides in Franklin, Tennessee, with her husband, three children, and four rescue dogs.

ABOUT THE ILLUSTRATOR

Bryan Langdo spent his childhood drawing dragons and ninjas on whatever was around—sketchbooks, math tests, desks. He studied under author/illustrator Robert J. Blake and then at the Art Students League of New York, where he focused on life drawing and portrait painting. After that he earned a BA in English from Rutgers College. Bryan is the illustrator of over thirty books. His picture book *Tornado Slim and the Magic Cowboy Hat* won a 2012 Spur Award for Storytelling from Western Writers of America. In addition to his work as an illustrator and writer, he works as an editor for an ESL website and app. Bryan lives in Hopewell, New Jersey, with his wife and two children. When not working, he likes to be in the woods.